BOSS FOR a WEEK

Ashton Scholastic Ltd.
165 Marua Rd, Panmure, Auckland, New Zealand

Ashton Scholastic Pty Ltd.
Lisarow, Box 579, Gosford NSW 2250, Australia

Scholastic Publications Ltd,
Holly Walk, Leamington Spa, Warwickshire CV32 4LS,
England

Scholastic Inc,
730 Broadway, New York NY 10003, USA

Scholastic-TAB Publications Ltd,
123 Newkirk Road, Richmond Hill,
Ontario L4C 3G5, Canada

National Library of New Zealand
Cataloguing-in-Publication data

HANDY, Libby:
    Boss for a Week / Story by Libby Handy
Pictures by Jack Newnham – (Auckland):
Ashton Scholastic, (1982). – 1 v.
    Children's story.
    ISBN 0-908643-01-2
    J823
    I Newnham, Jack II. Title

8765   9/8   0123/9

First published 1982 by Ashton Scholastic Limited, Auckland, New Zealand

for Caroline

Printed in Hong Kong

BOSS for a WEEK

story by
Libby Handy
pictures by
Jack Newnham

Ashton
Scholastic

LOLLIPOP POWER NOW!

If I were boss on MONDAY
in our house,
in our house,
I'd make this rule:

All people living here
coming in from work or
school must change their
clothes IMMEDIATELY!
(NO bare feet either.)

But...

5

... little Caroline,
sweet Caroline,
neat and natty darlin' Caroline,
may go straight out to play.

8

If I were boss
on TUESDAY
    in our house,
    in our house,
I'd proclaim:

All people living here
must be inside this
house by five o'clock
ON THE DOT !

    Except for...

9

...little Caroline,
sweet Caroline,
prompt and punctual
darlin' Caroline.
She may stay out later.

(Even if it gets a little dark.)

If I were boss on WEDNESDAY
    in our house,
    in our house,
I'd insist:

All people sitting at the
table about to eat
must get up and wash their
hands — and faces too.
(And their knees.)

        EVERYONE except...

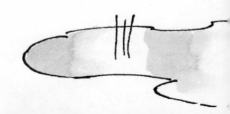

13

... little Caroline,
sweet Caroline,
clean and gleaming
darlin' Caroline.

She may start
her dinner.

If I were boss on THURSDAY
in our house,
in our house,
I'd announce loud and clear:

If Dad's got the leftover
meatloaf in his sandwiches
for lunch,
then...

little Caroline,
sweet Caroline,
hungry, STARVING,
darlin' Caroline,
she shall have the same.

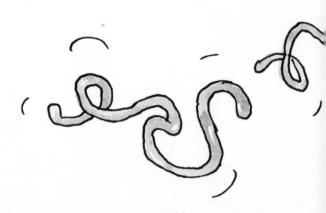

(Certainly **NOT** spaghetti !)

If I were boss on FRIDAY
in our house,
in our house,
I'd tell them straight:

All people not having to
attend school tomorrow may
stay up as long as they like
and watch
television.

Especially...

...little Caroline,
sweet Caroline,
perky, wide-awake,
darlin' Caroline.

(She may
choose the
channel
too.)

If I were boss on SATURDAY
   in our house,
   in our house,
I'd instruct the grown-ups:

No chores for
kids today—
no making beds,
doing dishes,
hanging out clothes
or dusting.

Anyway, NOT for...

23

She needs her rest.

If I were boss on SUNDAY
in our house,
in our house,
everyone would
know:

WHO gets the wishbone
and the biggest heap
of ice-cream — two helpings!

Who but...

... little Caroline,
sweet Caroline,
always-eats-her-dinner-up,
darlin' Caroline.

(And it's not conditional on eating her vegetables either!)

If I were boss
for just one week
    in our house,
    in our house,
I'd make them change their ways:
And all for little Caroline,
sweet Caroline,
that golden headed angel,
that paragon of virtue,
that beautiful,
wonderful,
marvellous she,

that dearest darlin', ...

. . . . ME!